RAIN
DROP
SPLASH

STORY BY ALVIN TRESSELT

PICTURES BY LEONARD WEISGARD

LOTHROP, LEE & SHEPARD CO   NEW YORK

Drip drop splash,
drip drop splash,
drip drop splash
went the rain all day.

Dripped from the shiny leaves, dropped from a rabbit's nose, splashed from a brown bear's tail.

Fell from a
daisy's face,
trickled down
the tree trunks,
and splunked
on a green
frog's back.

There were so many rain drops
they made a puddle.
The puddle grew larger, and
larger, and larger, until it
became a pond. Water-lilies
floated on it, little fish
swam in it, and tiny snails
sat beside it.

Still it rained. Drip
drop splash, drip drop splash,
drip drop splash.
The little pond grew larger and
larger and spilled right over
into a brook.

Tumbling
and splashing
and running down
the mountain. Scared
a chipmunk, splashed
some violets, passed a
mother deer showing her
baby how to drink.

Jumped over big stones, fell into deep pools, and rested on a bed of soft green moss. Then tumbled into a lake.

Now it was a big lake, with big fish and tall pickerel weed. Dragonflies skimmed over

the water, turtles floated quietly, and a red winged blackbird built his nest in the rushes.

Still it rained. Drip drop splash,
drip drop splash, drip drop splash.
The lake grew larger and larger.
It flooded a farmer's meadow
and the cows stood in the mud.

It covered a road
and the cars couldn't pass
and the children
had to go to school in a boat.

Then it overflowed into a river,
with houses and towns along the
shore. It ran under bridges and

over waterfalls. Men fished
from the rocks, and two
teams had a boat race.

Past factories and warehouses, the river came to great cities with docks. There were ships and barges

and scows and tankers, and a
boatful of people
on a holiday.

Little boys jumped into the water,
subway trains and cars
ran under it, ferry boats puffed
back and forth on top,
and seagulls flew over it
looking for fish to eat.

Then it passed a fort
and a lighthouse and a bell buoy,
and the river flowed into the sea.

Tall waves rolled up
to meet it.
There was an ocean liner
with lots of little tug boats
guiding it. The sun came out,
and at last the rain stopped.